① 引子讲。

③ 开场介绍回

对接包

④ ① 写场 { 外望—读
教师—讲改
10岁—抱读明白

② → 咖啡
姐姐 PoLA

PoLA

① 1. where is my shoes ?   I don't know
Don't you have 2eye ?

② 2. what what is your Qu
② what your
where is my Pen ?   I don't know
why do I know your pen ?

3. Daddy This is my friend   She lookup to him + little boy
(= little)
她 told won

4. sisters sister calling with someone   说话, fast ( )
5. good for travelling. want to pee.
try to see artself   → ,explain tooheng
want to pee, standup.

Me Too!

Jamie Harper

 LITTLE, BROWN AND COMPANY

New York ∾ Boston

170201

For Grace

First Edition

Little, Brown and Company

Time Warner Book Group
1271 Avenue of the Americas, New York, NY 10020
Visit our Web site at www.lb-kids.com

Library of Congress Cataloging-in-Publication Data

Harper, Jamie.
    Me Too!/Jamie Harper — 1st ed.
        p. cm.
    Summary: The only time Grace can get away from her little sister, who copies her every move, is when she goes to swimming class.
    ISBN 0-316-60552-2
    [1. Sisters—Fiction. 2. Imitation—Fiction. 3. Interpersonal relations—Fiction. 4. Swimming—Fiction]
I. Title.
PZ7.H23134Me 2004
[E]—dc21   2002043340

10 9 8 7 6 5 4 3 2 1

TWP

Printed in Singapore

The illustrations for this book were done in ink and watercolor on Fabriano paper.
The text was set in Caslon 540, and the display type is Spumoni.

There were two words that drove Grace crazy.
Her sister, Lucy, never said anything else.
Whatever Grace did, Lucy did too.

She dressed like Grace.

She ate her breakfast like Grace.

She even sat on the potty like Grace.

And every morning she tried to go to school with Grace.

"Monkey see,
monkey do,"
smiled her parents.

"She copies you because she loves you, Gracie," said her mother.
"Because she wants to be like you," said her father.
"Can't she learn to say something else?!" asked Grace.

Before she got on the bus, Grace said to Lucy,
"*STOP it right now*, or I'll put you in the closet
without Gorilly or your binkies for as long as you live!"
But Lucy didn't hear.

When Grace had a playdate, Lucy had one.

When Grace went to swim class, Lucy went.

When Grace joined Junior Scouts, Lucy joined.

Me Too!

And every evening when Grace went to bed, Lucy did too.

"Monkey see, monkey do," chimed her parents.
"She thinks you're wonderful," said her mother.
"She wants to BE you," said her father.
"I have absolutely NO privacy," said Grace. And she didn't.

Wherever Grace went, Lucy went too.
Downstairs, upstairs—*everywhere*!
To secret places, even private places.

Me Too!

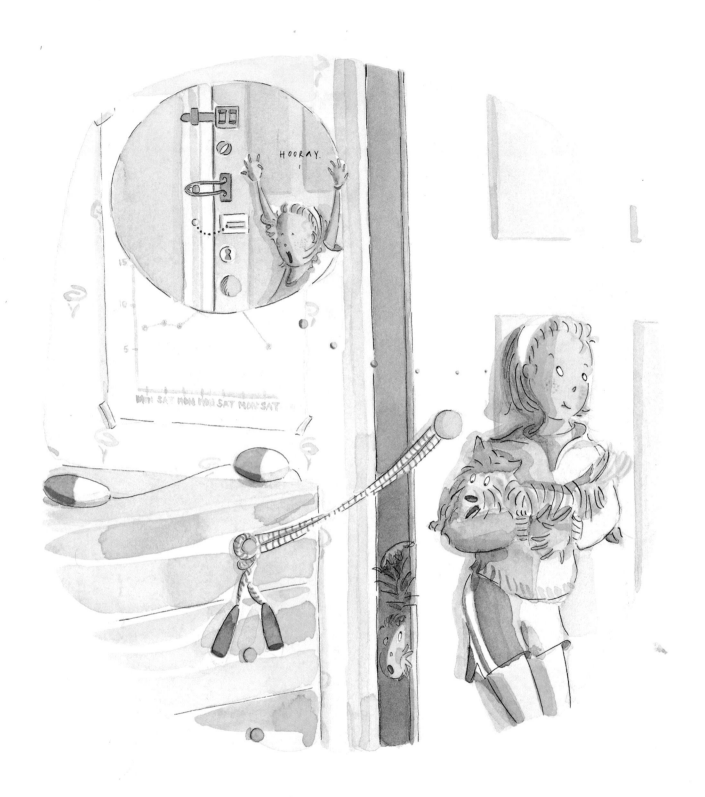

All Grace wanted was a lock on her door.
"It's just not safe," said her mother.
"You could get locked in there all by yourself," said her father.
Grace thought that sounded like a great idea.

One afternoon, when Grace's mother came to pick her up from school, Lucy came too.

"LOOK," said Edna, pointing. "It's a mini Grace!"

"Monkey see,
monkey do,"
squealed the Taylor twins.
Everyone started giggling.

Grace grabbed Lucy's
lunchbox and backpack.
"C'mon Lucy," she said.
"It's time for your afternoon nap.
Too bad your blankie's in
the washing machine.
I hope it doesn't get stuck."

When they got home, Grace ran upstairs crying.
She stopped in front of Lucy's room and then
slipped inside. A few seconds later, she dashed out,
squeezing Gorilly in one hand and a bunch of
binkies in the other.

Monkey see,
Monkey do.
See, her toes!
I'll paint yours blue.

Monkey see,
Monkey do.
He has spots.
Now you do too.

Monkey see,
Monkey do.
Oops, your bow.
I need some glue.

That afternoon, Grace was sent to The Rocker for a full hour.

On Saturday, Grace had swim class.
She couldn't wait to get to the pool.
She loved to swim.

And she loved her swim coach, Miss Finn, even more.

BUBBLES
UP!

Miss Finn could do everything.
She was in tip-top shape.
She could hold her breath under water
for more than two minutes.
And she could do a perfect swan dive.

"Call me Coach," she said,
"because we are a team of serious athletes."

When it came to aquatics
trivia, Coach Finn knew it all.

/əˈkwætɪk/

/ˈtrɪviə/ 琐事

FINN FACT NO. 36

THE AVERAGE PERSON
PRODUCES ENOUGH SPIT
IN A LIFETIME TO FILL
TWO WHOLE SWIMMING POOLS.

WHO KNEW?

SHE'S SO SMART.

GRACE

WOW.

Class began that morning with an underwater bubble-blowing drill.
"Bubbles up!" Grace cheered from the side.

While Coach Finn was busy, Grace addressed the class.
"Did you know that elephants can swim twenty miles a day?
They use their trunks as natural snorkels," she said.
But no one answered.

Coach Finn saved the last five minutes for free swim.
Grace wanted to try a swan dive. She placed her toes
carefully over the edge of the pool, tucked her chin down,
and pushed off.

Grace gulped. She coughed.
Then she swallowed some more of the pool.
Her body was stinging all over and she felt horrible.
She climbed out of the water and disappeared into her towel.

"Nice dive," said Edna, "looked more like a belly flop to me."
"Wow," said Frank, "I bet that really hurt. Why'd you do it?"
"That's SO obvious," said Edna. "Grace wants to be just like Coach Finn. She's a copycat."

"You're right, Edna!" said Coach Finn.
"Grace and I do like a lot of the same things.
We're always trading swim facts in the locker room,
and I love her sense of style."
Everyone stared at Grace with envy.

In the car on the way home, Grace was quiet.
Not Frank. He had a lot to say.
"Wow, Grace, Coach Finn *really* likes you.
Are you going to be a swim coach one day?"

Later that evening when the girls were taking a bath,
Lucy grabbed a pair of Grace's goggles and tried to put them on.

This time, Grace looked on. She didn't say a word.
And before Lucy could cry "Me too!" Grace said,
"It's all right, I'll help you."

She pulled the goggles
carefully over Lucy's face,
stretching them into perfect position.

"I've got something I want
to show you," Grace said.
"Jump in."

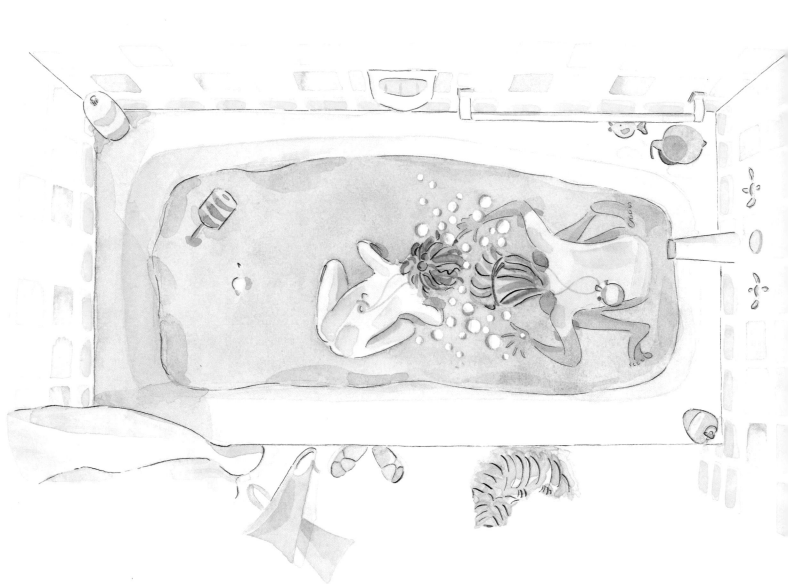

And of course, Lucy did.

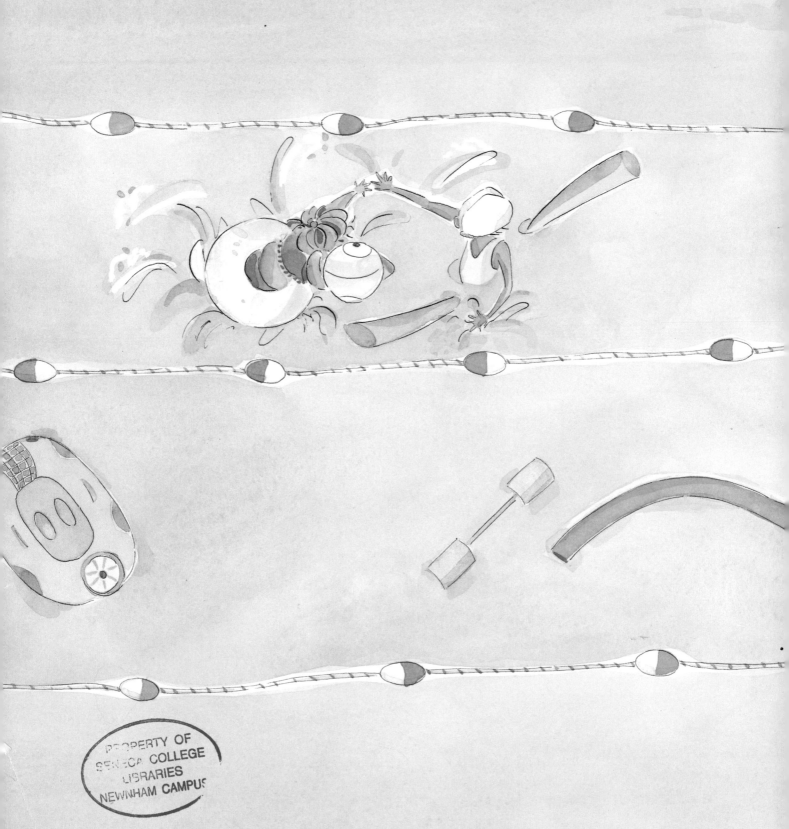